ALIEN ATTACK
CHAPTER 1
A CLOSE ENCOUNTER

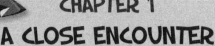

VICTOR VOLT, one of U.Z.Z.'s Top Agents, is **hunched** over his **Sky Bike**, speeding through the night sky at what would be a recklessly *HIGH SPEED* if he wasn't in white hot pursuit of a flying saucer. No, he's not officiating a tea party at a care home for retired delinquents. This flying saucer is an actual extraterrestrial spacecraft! A *U.F.O.!

*U.F.O. – in this instance, an Unidentified Flying Object. But in another context, in the periodical known as The Animal Alliance Quarterly, for example, it could be referring to the United Federation of Ostriches. It's well worth keeping on the right side of this particular U.F.O. as it is well known that there is nothing more obstreperous than an ostracized ostrich.

ALIEN ATTACK

Close behind Victor is **ANITA KNIGHT** – the fastest U.Z.Z. Top Agent on no wheels. She is powering forward through the night air on her **Sky Bike.** She is gaining on Victor as he gains on the alien spaceship.

"We're gaining on it!" gasps Anita, into her Communicator.

She is talking to **PROFESSOR PROFESSOR** – originally from Bavaria but now residing in U.Z.Z.'s top secret headquarters from where he is now monitoring the progress of U.Z.Z.'s two Top Agents. **PROFESSOR PROFESSOR** is U.Z.Z.'s principal boffin and pioneer in the field of thinking "outside of his box".

BE CAREFUL, ANITA!

says **PROFESSOR PROFESSOR**, as he tracks the progress of the spacecraft.

The

Fluffy Bunny

Show

Book Two
Snookums and the Bunnies
Form a Band

Fluffy Bunny fans. **Sweet Little Granny** here. Welcome to yet another lovely Fluffy Bunny Book. Before we begin – shall we sing our song?
NO!
Okay! ... Oh. What do mean, "No?" Oh, dear...

ALIEN ATTACK

"ZE ALIEN IS TRAVELLING VERY FAST IN ZE DIRECTION OF ZE HARBOUR!"

"Don't worry, Professor Professor," says Victor. "We've got it in our sights." He narrows his eyes in the direction of his intended **TARGET** and eases down on the accelerator of his **Sky Bike**, pushing its *turbo-charged* engine to the limit. As he **ZooMS** along, he says to Anita, "Cool! A real life alien!"

Victor and Anita guide their **Sky Bikes** in the direction of the harbour, **skirting** around the beach, shooting along a jetty and then *zipping* between the masts of a **JUMBLE** of luxury yachts. The boats are left **bobbing** and **swaying** in the ocean, their masts clacking together, in the wake of the speeding **Sky Bikes.**

ALIEN ATTACK

The alien spaceship is skimming the ocean just metres above the surface.

Its **pulsing**, coloured lights are reflected on the black sea below. It's a hard line to hold,

even for an ultra manoeuvrable space vehicle.

The alien spaceship hits an unexpected breaker and begins bouncing across the surface of the water like a skimming stone.

Careering

out OF control

the spinning disc knocks a chunk out of the waves…

One… Two… Three times.

And then…

BOUNCE…

With one last enormous

THUNK!

ALIEN ATTACK

The flying saucer stops dead in the sand on the beach of a small, isolated, tropical island, several kilometres out to sea.

Sneck!

A crack, caused by the impact, appears in the hull of the spacecraft.

OOOOOoooovvvvv...

The spaceship's engines die and its coloured lights flicker out, leaving it in darkness.

Anita and Victor are travelling so fast they shoot past the island. They have to turn a large circle in the air in order to slow down and double back to the island. The flying saucer has bitten the sand and looks as inconspicuous now as a child's toy left outside in the sandpit overnight.

ALIEN ATTACK

The two Agents touch down on the beach.
As their **Sky Bikes** wind down, the only
sounds are the gentle lapping of the waves on
the shore and the faint hiss of the spaceship
as **WISPS** of steam rise from the crack in its
darkened shell.

"Oh no," sighs Victor, jumping down from his
Sky Bike and creeping towards the defunct
spacecraft. "I think it's a goner."
"Are you sure?" says Anita. She also climbs
down from her **Sky Bike**, but she hangs
back a bit, not sure what to expect. Victor
moves forward and tentatively reaches out a
hand towards the blackened pod...

VVVVVOOOOOOOOOOO!

The U.F.O.* powers back up again – lights
pulsing, engine humming and whirring.

ALIEN ATTACK

*U.F.O. – in this instance, an Unidentified Flying Object. But in another context, for example the Journal of Gastronomy, it could be referring to an Unpleasantly Fizzy Oyster – the consumption of which can lead to many disagreeable side effects including sickness, dizzy spells and the production of pearls.

Victor jumps back from the spacecraft, letting out an embarrassingly girly scream...

"Aiiieee...!"

...that he tries to turn into a manly cough.

"...AHEM-HEM-HEM."

Fooling no one.

"Are you OK?" Anita asks.

"Yes, yes," says Victor, blushing. "Completely fine. Which is more than can be said for the little guy in there, by the looks of things!"

ANiTA KNiGHT and **ViCTOR VOLT** lean in towards the glass bubble on top of the spacecraft and peer inside – becoming the first humans to get a glimpse of an actual alien life form.

ALIEN ATTACK

CHAPTER 2
FIRST CONTACT

"Veeeeeeet cooooo de-vvvUmmmmm!" says the little alien, inside its glass bubble on top of its spacecraft.

"Veeeeeeet cooooo de-vvvUmmmmm!" it says, again.

Top U.Z.Z. Agents **ANITA KNIGHT** and **VICTOR VOLT** are on a deserted desert island in the middle of the night. And they are looking upon a **REAL, LIVE ALIEN**. Something humankind has dreamt about for thousands of years. A thing almost beyond imagining.

So what does it look like…? Well… It's green and looks a bit like a jelly worm from the pick 'n' mix sweet counter at the cinema.

"Go on!" says Anita, nudging Victor towards the U.F.O*. "Make 'first contact'!"

*U.F.O. – in this instance, an Unidentified Flying Object. But in another context, in the New Mother's Handbook for example, it could be referring to Unnaturally Fluorescent Oranges – that is, balls that have found their way into the fruit bowl and could, unless otherwise identified, be mistaken for something suitable for juicing.

"OK," says Victor, a little nervous. He clears his throat – "Ahem!" – and kneels down in the sand. He bends the index finger of his right hand and uses the knuckle to tap on the glass. Victor puts on a friendly voice and says, "Hey there, little fella!"

"Veeeeeeet cooooo de-vvvUmmmmm!" says the little alien, bashing some kind of communication device as though it might be trying to call for help. **"Veeeeeeet cooooo de-vvvUmmmmm!"**

Anita stifles a guffaw.
"'Hey there, little fella!'?" she mocks.
"What?" says Victor, annoyed.
"What's wrong with that?"
Anita chuckles and says, "This is a big moment for humankind and you say, 'Hey there, little fella!'? Heheheh!"
Victor stands up. "Well, OK, Miss **'GIANT LEAP FOR HUMANKIND'!** You give it a go."
"OK!" says Anita. "I will!"

Anita approaches the crash-landed spaceship.
She clears her throat.
"Ahem!" – and raises a hand.
"I bet she says 'Greetings'!"
Victor grumbles, under his breath.
"Greetings!" trills Anita.

ALIEN ATTACK

"HAH!" scoffs Victor.

"What?" says Anita, annoyed.

"Skee-ooh-oow!"

That's a wave of feedback from the alien spacecraft. The force of the noise knocks Anita and Victor backwards.

"Ooof!"

That's Anita and Victor falling backwards. A door slides open on the side of the U.F.O.* and an orb on a stalk pops out.

*U.F.O. - in this instance, an Unidentified Flying Object. But in another context, such as the Little Book of Animal Stereotypes, for example, it could be referring to an Ultra Flash Otter - an ostentatious otter who can be spotted taking wads of cash out of the river bank and swanning around in designer labels. (See also Super Charged Platypus.)

The alien clears its throat – "Ahem!" – and
the orb, obviously some sort of translating
device, pulsates with light as it converts the
alien's voice into English.

"Ahem!" crackles the translating device.

"Veeeeeeet cooooo de-vvvUmmmmm!"
says the alien.

This comes through the translator as,
"Greetings!"

Anita grins and steps forward.

"Greetings!" she says.

Victor rolls his eyes. "Well," he says, "at least
it didn't say, 'Take me to your leader'!"

"Spling-ba-te," says the alien,
"boooooooo-ing-vvv!"

This twangs out of the translator as,
"Take me to your leader!"

CHAPTER 3
SIIIIING-BOOO-DONG VIUUU

Top U.Z.Z. Agents **ANiTA KNi9HT** and **ViCToR VolT** and their follically challenged, mono-browed brainiac colleague **PROFESSOR PROFESSOR** are sitting together in the drawing room of the Head of U.Z.Z. – **A MAN SO IMPORTANT HIS NAME IS "CHANGED DAILY"**. In the middle of them all is the alien – still inside its spaceship bubble, the translator device already out and ready to… er… translate!

"Congratulations, team," says their leader proudly, "on recovering our very first alien visitor!"
"Veeeeeeet cooooo de-vvvUmmmmm," says the alien, **"kooooooo-ing-vvv!"**
The orb pulsates and translates,
"Greetings, leader!"
"Ah, no!" protests the Head of U.Z.Z. gently. "I am not our leader. My name, for reasons of

security is changed daily and today you
may call me..."

BEEP!

A text comes through on his mobile. He takes
his phone from his pocket and squints at the
screen. He groans. **"'Peekaboo'."**

"Heheheh!" snicker Anita, Victor and
PROFESSOR PROFESSOR.
"Heheheh!" cackles the Alien.
"Heheheh!" crackles the translating device.

"Our World Leader will be informed of your
arrival," says **Peekaboo,** brusquely, "and a
meeting will be arranged!"
"Siiiiing-booo-dong viUUU, Zee-bay-voo!"
says the Alien.
The pulsating orb translates,
"Thank you, 'Peekaboo'!"

ALiEN ATTACK

Yes, aliens exist and, yes, they are green! Today the World Leader and her husband will meet the Alien Ambassador - live on world television. History will be historifying right before your eyes tonight at ten! You may be you, but I'm Stacey Stern!

Marlon Zen, a presenter of television makeover shows, has floppy hair and even floppier hands. His hands are flip-flopping all over the place as he says, "This is history, people! History! And tonight we'll make it stylish history!"

Marlon Zen steps down from the stage on which the World Leader is due to meet the Alien in just a few short hours. He can hardly contain himself at the excitement of it all. His **TROUSERS** have never been so immaculately **CREASED**, while his face remains suspiciously line-free.

"Calm. Calm. Calm," Marlon repeats to himself as he takes dinky steps backstage. *"I am Marlon and I am calm."*

Yes, Marlon is holding himself together in a very calm and dignified fashion – and fashion is what he is all about. That is, until he finds himself standing right next to the World Leader and her husband.

"Oooh, World Leader…" giggles Marlon Zen… And one can only imagine what he was about to say next because **Peekaboo** interrupts him. "World Leader!" he commands. "And World

Leader's husband! Remove your heads!"

The World Leader and her husband remove their heads and Marlon **KEELS OVER IN A DEAD FAINT.** Except it's not really the World Leader and her husband, it's Top Agents **ANITA KNIGHT** and **VICTOR VOLT** in World Leader and husband costumes!

"Is he OK?" asks Anita, looking down at Marlon who is out cold.

"Perhaps I should have explained to him," says Peekaboo. "The security risk is too great for the real World Leader and her husband to attend. They are following events from an airtight bunker in `Helsinki`."

ALIEN ATTACK

Marlon Zen comes round, rubbing his eyes in disbelief.

"Victor and Anita," says Peekaboo, "Marlon will now prepare you for the ceremony. Good luck!"

Anita is relaxing on a settee. She's wearing her World Leader costume minus the head that, rather disturbingly, she's left in the fruit bowl on the coffee table.

Meanwhile, Marlon Zen is putting Victor through his paces. Victor is wearing his World Leader's husband costume minus the head that, even more disturbingly, he's left in the biscuit jar.

"You have to greet the alien in its own language, Victor," says Marlon.

ALIEN ATTACK

"*She can do it,*" he says, nodding towards Anita. "*So you should be able to do it too.*" Anita smiles, smugly, and sticks out her not-so-alien tongue at her fellow agent.

"OK, OK," says Victor. "I'll have another go."

"*Right,*" says Marlon. "*Repeat after me!*"

"Veeeeeeet cooooo de-vvvUmmmmm."

"Veeeeeeet cooooo de-wub..."

says Victor. "Oh! That wasn't right. Let me try again. OK." He shakes himself out, stretches his mouth, wiggles his tongue and exhales a few times.

"Right then. Ready. Here goes…"

"*Get on with it!*" says Marlon, tetchily.

"Veeeeeet cooooo de-vvvUmmmmm," says Victor.

"*Brilliant,*" says Marlon. "*Now you've said 'Greetings' in alien. Now you have to say its name.*

"La-oooooo-thrrruuup."

(This last bit ends with a **raspberry**. As Marlon does it, little flecks of spit land on Victor's face.)

Victor wipes his face with the cuff of his sleeve – or, rather, the cuff of his World Leader's husband's disguise sleeve.

ALIEN ATTACK

"La-ooooooo-thrrruuUp!"

says Victor, making sure he leans in real close to Marlon when he does the final raspberry.

"Alright! Alright!" says Marlon, wiping his face with the sleeve of his shirt.

Anita rolls her eyes. "Boys!" she sighs.

Suddenly, the brass bright blare of a bugle fanfare makes them all look up.

TA-DA-DAN-DAN-DAN-DAAA!

(That was the fanfare.)

"Quick!" says Anita. "The ceremony's starting!"

ALIEN ATTACK

"Argh!" wails Marlon, in a blind panic.
"Where are your heads? Get your heads!
Where are your heads?"
"Here's mine!" says Anita, picking her false
World Leader head out of the fruit bowl.
"Where's mine?" says Victor.
"I can't remember!"

cries an unsuspecting U.Z.Z. Agent who
fancies a biscuit and finds the World Leader's
husband's head, instead, inside the biscuit jar.
"Oh, yes," Victor blushes, "I knew I'd left it
somewhere safe!"

ALIEN ATTACK

Marlon's running backwards and forwards like a headless chicken.

"*Where's my head?*" he yelps. "*My head! My head! Where is it? Oh –*" He stops dead in his tracks.

That's right, I've got it on.

CHAPTER 4
ROYAL FLUSH

Marlon Zen, his hair immaculately coiffed and his cheeks glowing with the slightest touch of rouge, takes to the stage just before ten o'clock. He is a picture of unshakable calm. "And now, ladies and gentlemen," he proclaims through the microphone and into the homes of millions of people worldwide,

"history shall be made!"

Marlon sashays down from the stage as two hydraulic walkways glide into place. On one walkway, the alien still in its spacecraft. On the other walkway, Top U.Z.Z. Agents ANITA KNIGHT and VICTOR VOLT in disguise.

"And here is the World Leader and her husband," commentates Marlon Zen, "moving towards what must surely be one of the most important meetings in the history of television meetings." Anita and Victor, disguised as the World Leader and her husband, raise their right arms and attempt a greeting in alien tongue. **"Veeeeeeet cooooo de-vvvUmmmmm,"** they both say. (Which, as we well know by now, means 'Greetings'!) And then, **"La-oooooooo-thrrruuup!"** (And **La-oooooooo-thrrruuup** of course, is the name of the alien.)

ALIEN ATTACK

"La-ooooooo-thrrruuup," replies in perfect English, "Greetings, World Leader and husband."

"*And now,*" commentates Marlon Zen, "*the moment we've all been waiting for. First contact between human and alien shall be made!*"

The glass bubble on top of the alien spaceship pops open with a hiss, and then slides slowly back. Steam **wafts** into the air around the nose of the supposed World Leader.

"Mmm!" thinks Anita, in her disguise as the World Leader. "What a delicious smell! Like... roast chicken!"

"A single touch of the World Leader's little finger against the tail of the alien is the agreed-upon greeting," comments Marlon, in hushed tones.

Anita reaches out with a trembling hand. Disguised as the World Leader and with the eyes of the world's population trained on her, all she can think is, "Yummy! Roast chicken!" Anita's little finger touches the alien's tail...

36

then she grabs the alien, stuffs it in her mouth

and **SUCKS IT UP** like a piece of spaghetti.

"SLUUUUUUURRRRRRRP!" says Anita, smacking her lips. **"DELICIOUS!"**

CHAPTER 5
MEAL DEAL

"Oh, Peekaboo!" says Marlon Zen, *swooning* into Peekaboo's arms.

"Oh, Anita!" says Victor, disguised as the World Leader's husband, as he drags Anita offstage.

"OH, LEDERUNTERHOSEN!" says **PROFESSOR PROFESSOR** as he watches the whole thing on a monitor.

Victor is backstage, having removed his World Leader's husband disguise. "Anita!" he says. "What have you done?"

"I'll tell you what she's done," barks Peekaboo, depositing an out cold Marlon on a nearby couch,

"she's triggered the invasion of the Earth!"

39

And, sure enough, by consulting his bank of
monitors, **PROFESSOR PROFESSOR** can confirm
that the...

EARTH iS NOW SURROUNDED BY ALiEN SPACECRAFT.

Ooops!

Anita begins to come round from her
post-dinner nap.

"What happened?" she asks, wiping a smear of
DROOL from the side of her mouth.

"You ate the alien live on world television!"
says Victor.
"Do you mind lowering your voice to a scream,"
says Anita, "and telling me what
really happened?"

But he doesn't need to. Because at exactly
that moment Anita sees the whole thing,
being repeated on world TV. What she
sees, in ultra close-up and super **slooow
moootiooon** is this:

Anita.

Disguised as the World Leader.

Grabbing the alien.

Stuffing it in her mouth.

And sucking it up.

Like a piece of spaghetti.

ALIEN ATTACK

"SLUUUUUUUUUUUUUUUUUUUUUUUUUURRRRRRRRRRRRRRRRRRRRRRRRRPP!"

Alien spacecraft are sliding out landing gear and touching down all over the surface of the Earth. And everywhere a spacecraft lands, the glass bubble pops open with a hiss. And as the glass glides back, steam curls into the air around the noses of whoever might be standing by and they think: "Oooh! Yummy roast beef!"

Or: "Hey! Fried chicken!"

Or: "Mmm! Sticky spare ribs!"

Or: "Lovely! A nice meat pie!"

Or: "Och! Haggis!"

Or: "Aaah! Cornish pasty!"

And this is inevitably followed by: "**SLUUUUUUURRRRRRRRP!**
Smashing!"

Or: "**SLUUUUUUURRRRRRRRP!** Alright!"

Or: "**SLUUUUUUURRRRRRRRP!** Scrummy!"

Or: "**SLUUUUUUURRRRRRRRP!** Brilliant!"

Or: "**SLUUUUUUURRRRRRRRP!** Pukka!"

PROFESSOR PROFESSOR consults the
monitors in front of him at U.Z.Z.'s top secret
headquarters.
"EVERYVUN IS EATING ZE ALIENS!" he squawks. "ANITA
VAS NOT ALONE IN FINDING ZEM IRRESISTIBLE!"
"Great!" says Victor, looking on the bright side.
"Then the battle's over. We win!"
"Not quite," says Anita.

ALIEN ATTACK

"**AAARRRGGGHHH!**" screams Victor, as he takes in Anita's appearance. "**A SPOTTY, BIG HAND THING!**"

Anita is covered in gaudy purple spots and her hands have grown to giant proportions!

Peekaboo's face appears on one of **PROFESSOR PROFESSOR'S** monitors.

"We have to stop the aliens coming to our planet!" he says.

"Everyone who eats one turns into a **spotty, big hand thing...**"

But he's suddenly distracted. "Oooh!" he says, and then

he sniffs. "Is that minted roast lamb I can smell...? With lashings of gravy...?"

"NO!" says **PROFESSOR PROFESSOR**. "IT'S BEEF SCHNITZEL!"

"**SLUUUUUURRRRRRRP!**" goes Peekaboo. "Tasty!"

"**SLUUUUUURRRRRRRP!**" goes **PROFESSOR PROFESSOR**. "SCHNITZEL-Y!"

"Victor," says Anita, scratching a particularly lurid spot on her forehead with an especially enlarged finger, "how come you can resist that wonderful smell?"

"I don't know," says Victor, thinking.

Then, suddenly, he gets it! "I know why I'm not affected!" he yelps, punching the air.

Victor knows why the yummy-smelling aliens do not affect him – and he knows just what to do to save humankind from becoming spotty, big hand things!

"THE FATE OF THE WORLD," says Victor, in an important voice,

"IS IN THE HANDS OF...VEGETARIANS!"

"SLUUUUUUURRRRRRRP!"

ALIEN ATTACK

CHAPTER 6
THE VEGETARIAN STRIKES BACK

Top U.Z.Z. **AGENT VICTOR VOLT, SPECIAL AGENT RAY**, and a couple of other U.Z.Z. Agents circle the alien mothership on **totally untested and highly dangerous**, specially-adapted-for-space **Sky Bikes**. Victor has assembled a **VEGETARIAN TASK FORCE**. Their mission: to save the entire world – including his close friends and colleagues **ANITA KNIGHT, PROFESSOR PROFESSOR** and **Peekaboo** from eminently edible aliens that turn human beings into spotty, big hand things!

Inside the mothership,
Victor and his
VEGETARIAN TASK FORCE
approach one of the aliens.

Victor's Communicator is turned to translate.

"Hold it right there!" says Victor, into his
Communicator.

"Argh!" says the alien, understandably
surprised.

"Is there any antidote to what you have done to
the human race?" enquires Victor, and he holds
the Communicator up to the alien.

"Yes!" says the alien, quite frankly.

ALIEN ATTACK

"We have been trying to tell you!
All you have to do is –"

But that's as far the alien gets because **SPECIAL AGENT RAY** has grabbed the alien…

"Erk!"

…and
scoffed him!

"**SLUUUUUUURRRRRRRP!**" goes **SPECIAL AGENT RAY**.
"Salty!"

"Ray!" squeals Victor. "What are you doing?
That alien was about to give us the antidote!"
"I'm sorry," says **SPECIAL AGENT RAY**. "It just
smelt so… fishy! I couldn't help myself!"
"I thought you were a vegetarian!" gasps
Victor. "Since when was a fish a vegetable?"
Victor slaps his forehead and shakes his head.
"OK, you guys – how many of you also eat fish?"

ALIEN ATTACK

After a bit of embarrassed shuffling and a few
"Ummms" and "Errrs" – one by one, each of
the other Agents puts up his or her hands.
Victor groans.

His Communicator beeps.

PROFESSOR PROFESSOR squawks,
**"Victor! Are you still
alive?"**

**"YES, I'M STILL
ALIVE,"** says Victor.
"Then look out of
the window,"
says **PROFESSOR PROFESSOR**,
"before you're not alive any
more!"

Victor moves towards the window of the alien
spaceship and peeps out.

"Oh no," he moans. "Another mothership!"

"To save confusion," **PROFESSOR PROFESSOR**
chunters on, "ve shall call ze ozzer
mozzership, ze fazzership."

Victor watches helplessly as the fathership
disgorges loads more little spaceships in the
direction of Earth.

"What are we going to do?" whimpers Victor.

"Victor!" squeals an Alien via Victor's
Communicator. "You can save your world
by – erk!"

"**SLUUUUUURRRRRRRP!**" goes a female U.Z.Z. Agent. *"Ocean pie!* My favourite!"

"Will you stop eating the aliens!" yells Victor.

"Victor! Victor!" screams another alien. "You can save your world by eating the – erk!"
"**SLUUUUUURRRRRRRP!**" goes another …Agent. *"Battered cod!* Yum yum!"

"Victor!" another alien jumps up and shouts into Victor's Communicator. "Eat the second course! Eat the – erk!"
"**SLUUUUUURRRRRRRP!**" goes yet another U.Z.Z. Agent.
"A fish finger and tomato sauce sandwich!"
Victor looks at him, darkly.
"Hey!" says the U.Z.Z. Agent, "I like fish finger and tomato sauce sandwiches!"

Victor shakes his head in despair. "'The second course'," he muses. "I wonder what was meant by that?"

ALIEN ATTACK

CHAPTER 7
JUST DESSERTS

As Top Agent **VICTOR VOLT** zips towards the fathership on his specially-adapted-for-space **Sky Bike**, it looks like it's up to him – and him alone – to save the entire population of Earth.

Behind him, his back-up crew of **SPECIAL AGENT RAY** and assorted U.Z.Z. Agents are struggling to steer their **Sky Bikes** with their absurdly large and spotty hands.
"Train your weapons at the fathership!" Victor cries.

"But," says **SPECIAL AGENT RAY**, into his Communicator, "it smells so chocolatey!"

"No!" says a female U.Z.Z. Agent. "Like hot rhubarb crumble – with cream!"

"No!" says another U.Z.Z. Agent. "More like... my mum's apple pie!"

"Or," says yet another U.Z.Z. Agent, "like strawberry fool!"

VICTOR VOLT is struck by a **BLINDING FLASH** of inspiration that almost knocks him off his souped-up **Sky Bike.**
"Wait!" he yells into his Communicator. "The second course! That's it! Lower your weapons everyone! Let them land!"

VICTOR VOLT and the other U.Z.Z. Agents board the fathership. It is stuffed with aliens – just like the green jelly ones, only these ones are yellow. A yellow alien talks to Victor via his Communicator.
"We have travelled many light years to see you," it says. "Have you eaten the green ones?"

"Yes," says Victor. "Well, I haven't but just about everyone else has. And they've all turned into spotty, big hand things!"

"Good!" says the yellow alien. "Now, to save your world you must – erk!"

"SLUUUUUURRRRRRP!"

goes **SPECIAL AGENT RAY**, gobbling down the yellow alien. "Mmm! Vanilla ice cream! And not the nasty cheap yellow kind, either, but the spendy white kind."

"SLUUUUUURRRRRRP!"

goes a female U.Z.Z. Agent.
"Treacle tart! Heavenly!"

"SLUUUUUURRRRRRP!"

goes another U.Z.Z. Agent.

"SLUUUUUUURRRRRRRP!"

Pineapple upside-down cake! I haven't had that for years!" goes yet another U.Z.Z. Agent. "Spotted dick with pink custard!"

Victor gives him a hard stare. "Hey!" he says,

"I LIKE SPOTTED DICK WITH PINK CUSTARD!"

And if you think this is all a bit too, too weird to swallow – just wait and see what happens next.

Ray starts to glow. His giant hands and his spotty skin begin to return to normal. He does a colossal belch...

"*BRAAAAAP!*"

...and a small blue alien, inside a bubble, comes out of his mouth.

"The fusion is complete," says the blue alien, in a calm and soothing voice.

 "Thank you, Earthling. Thank you for being part of our life cycle. Thank you for your acidic digestive juices."

"***BRAAAAAP!***" goes a female U.Z.Z. Agent.

"***BRAAAAAP!***" goes another U.Z.Z. Agent.

"***BRAAAAAP!***" goes yet another U.Z.Z. Agent.

Three more blue aliens appear and three more Agents return to normal.

And so it happens.

All around the Earth. People eat yellow aliens that smell like their favourite puddings. They burp up blue ones.

ALIEN ATTACK

"*BRAAAAAP!*"

goes **ANITA KNIGHT**. "Oh, sorry!"

"*BRAAAAAP!*"

goes Peekaboo. "Pardon me!"

"*BRAAAAAAP!*"

goes **PROFESSOR PROFESSOR**.

And they all return to normal.

U.Z.Z.'s Top Agents **ANITA KNIGHT** and **VICTOR VOLT** and **PROFESSOR PROFESSOR** (the brain behind numerous totally untested and highly dangerous inventions) are gathered together in the Drawing Room of U.Z.Z. headquarters. Peekaboo is in his usual spot, leaning casually against the mantelpiece.

"For centuries, mankind has sought the answer to the biggest question of all," he pontificates.
"Why are we here?"
Peekaboo looks around the room and studies the serious faces looking back.

"Well, now we know!" he says, firmly.
"Everybody comfortable with that?"
"Yep!" say Victor and Anita, at once.
"Fine by me."
"YUP," says **PROFESSOR PROFESSOR**.
"VERY COMFY."

"Good," says Peekaboo.

"*BRAAAAAP!*"

Victor is cranky when Anita mocks his "Hey there, little fella!" greeting to the alien.

In the Briefing Room, the alien thinks it is being introduced to the World Leader.

Marlon collapses in a faint when Anita takes off the head of her World Leader disguise.

The smell of the alien is too good to resist, so Anita sucks it up, live on television.

ALIEN ATTACK

Anita's full stomach triggers an alien invasion of the Earth!

After Anita digests the alien, she turns into a big, spotty hand thing!

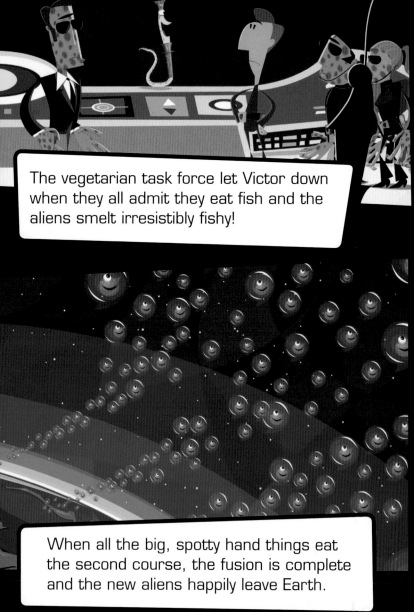

The vegetarian task force let Victor down when they all admit they eat fish and the aliens smelt irresistibly fishy!

When all the big, spotty hand things eat the second course, the fusion is complete and the new aliens happily leave Earth.

The disguised Professor Professor attempts to smash every single fake remote control Doctor Doctor has to hand.

But then she slips up and hands the real remote control to Anita. Oh dear.

Fluffy Bunny

Show

Book One

Foofy Bunkins

We interrupt this book to bring you an
IMPORTANT ANNOUNCEMENT!
DOCTOR DOCTOR HAS INVENTED A REMOTE CONTROL.

And not just any remote control! Doctor Doctor's remote control controls the Sun. Remotely. Two of U.Z.Z.'s Top Secret Agents are in hot pursuit, on a mission to retrieve and disable Doctor Doctor's dastardly device.

DESTINATION SUN
CHAPTER 1
VICTOR PUTS HIS FOOT IN IT

VICTOR VOLT sits proudly astride his **Sky Bike** his head down low over the handlebars as he *ZOOMS* through the city at incredibly high speed. **ANITA KNIGHT** clings on to her **Sky Bike**, her hair whipping out behind her as she executes a dramatic ninety-degree turn into a

perilously narrow passageway between two tall buildings. Together, they are on another life-threatening mission to...

save the World!

"Wahey!" says Anita.

"Whee!" says Victor.

If it sounds like they're having too much **FUN** to be on a life-threatening mission, that's because **you** haven't sped through the city on a **Sky Bike**. It's a pretty exhilarating ride. Even if **you** were about to crash headfirst into a wall, **you** would still be saying –

"Wahey!" says Anita.

"Whee!" says Victor.

And then the Sun goes out and the sky turns to black.

"Who turned out the lights?" says Victor, now sitting not so proudly astride the mangled wreck of his **Sky Bike.**

"Who said that?" says Anita, through the gloom. "Oh. I just did."

The Communicator on the twisted ruins of Anita's **Sky Bike** crackles into life. It's a much-needed message from HQ.

"VICTOR!" says PROFESSOR PROFESSOR. "ARE YOU STILL ALIVE?"

"Y-Y-Yes," shivers Victor, icicles appearing on his nose. **"I'm still alive!** And *f-f-freezing* to *d-d-death*!"

"How *c-c-come* it's so *c-c-cold* all of a sudden?" shudders Anita, icicles appearing on her eyelashes.

"It's Doctor Doctor's remote control," says **PROFESSOR PROFESSOR**, over the Communicator. "She's turned off the Sun!"

"We *m-m-must* find *D-D-Doctor D-D-Doctor*," stammers Victor, icicles appearing on his icicles... Oh, you get the picture!

"**Looking for something?**"

says **DOCTOR DOCTOR**, stepping out of the shadows with the remote control in her hand.

"**Get her!**" says **ANITA KNIGHT**, leaping into action. She's quick, but not as quick as **DOCTOR DOCTOR'S button finger!**

DOCTOR DOCTOR jabs a big red button on her remote

AND REACTIVATES THE SUN!

AAARGH!

Victor and Anita are dazzled by the brightness of the Sun's rays.

"Too bright for ya?" taunts **DOCTOR DOCTOR**, brandishing her button finger once again.

"Then how about this?"

AAARGH!

Victor and Anita are plummeted back into blackness.

And crash into one another.

"Ooof!"

And now what about this?
click
We've got to get hold of –
And this?
click
That remote control –
And this?
Before something –
click
And this?
Really terrible happens!
click
Ooops! I've dropped my remote control!

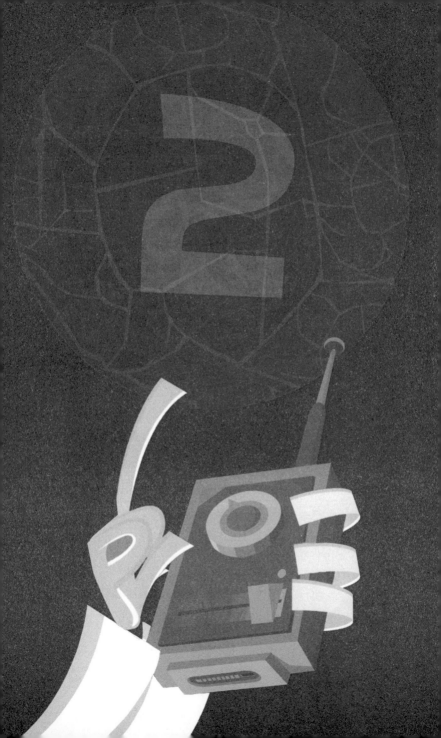

CHAPTER 2
THE END OF THE WORLD

With the Sun snuffed out, by Secret Agent **VICTOR VOLT**, the World, as we know it, is over. However, it's not all doom and gloom... Oh. Actually – it is. That was the news. You may be you, but I'm Stacey Stern. Thank you, and goodnight. **Forever**.

"I'VE DISMANTLED ZE REMOTE CONTROL," says **PROFESSOR PROFESSOR** in the Control Room of the U.Z.Z. top secret Secret Headquarters, "I HAVE LOOKED VERY CLOSELY AT EVERY DETAIL AND I HAVE MADE A VERY DEFINITE DISCOVERY."

"What is it?" asks Victor. "What have you discovered?"

"ZAT I DON'T HAVE ZE SLIGHTEST IDEA HOW ZIS CONTROLLED ZE SUN," shrugs **PROFESSOR PROFESSOR**.

"Victor!" gasps Anita, still annoyed with Victor for irreversibly switching off the Sun.

"You really put your **FOOT** in it this time!"

Victor puts his best argument forward. "It's not my fault!" he whines. "I didn't mean to tread on the remote control!"

Luckily, their tired argument is interrupted by a ringing.

Ring! Ring!

Ring! Ring!

"It's the T.H.E.M. phone!" shouts Anita.

Ring! Ring!

"I know," says **THE HEAD OF U.Z.Z. AND A MAN SO IMPORTANT HIS NAME IS "CHANGED DAILY".**

Ring! Ring!

"Answer it!" says Anita.

Ring! Ring!

"But what if it's T.H.E.M.?" says **CHANGED DAILY**, apprehensively.

Ring! Ring!

"Of course it's T.H.E.M.!" says Anita,

"It's the T.H.E.M. phone!"

Ring! Ring!

"Just answer it," sighs Victor.

CHANGED DAILY dries a sweaty palm on the leg of his trousers and picks up the phone. "Hello," he says, in his best phone answering voice. "U.Z.Z. here. Who may I say is calling, please?"

"I am **DOCTOR DOCTOR**," squawks **DOCTOR DOCTOR**, down the line. "Who are you?" "For reasons of security, my name is **CHANGED DAILY**," says the Head of U.Z.Z. "Today you may call me…" He presses a button on his phone and a text message beeps through. He opens the text message and reads it, carefully. "Um… **Oinky Doinky.**"

DOCTOR DOCTOR stifles a laugh before saying, "**Mr Doinky** – the reason I am calling is to suggest we..."

And here she leaves a pause for dramatic effect.

A long pause...

(Because there's a lot of drama.)

"...JOIN FORCES!"

"**GASP!**" gasps **Oinky Doinky**. "You're suggesting we **JOIN FORCES?**"

"Yes," says **DOCTOR DOCTOR** matter-of-factly. "When Victor trod on the remote control, the Sun went out."

"Oh, come on!" interrupts Victor. "It could have happened to anyone!"

"The Sun must be re-lit," proclaims **DOCTOR DOCTOR**. "Take me back to the Sun and I shall

SAVE THE EARTH from Victor's **terrible crime!**"

"Hey!" Victor jumps out of his chair to defend himself. "You were the one who invented a remote control that controls the Sun. Remotely."

"For the sake of the planet," interrupts **Oinky Doinky**. "We agree."

As if a journey to the Sun is not an **astonishing** and **electrifying** thing in itself –

iT WOULD APPEAR THAT U.Z.Z. iS To joiN FORCES WiTH T.H.E.M.!

Waking up on a regular day like today – who could have thought such an extraordinary thing would occur?

What other **SHOCKS** and **SURPRISES** could possibly be awaiting you, just over the page? There's only one way to find out...

Well, actually there are a couple of ways. You could ask someone who's read the book already. Or maybe you could treat this as a creative writing exercise and make up the next chapter yourself. But, really, the simplest solution would be to just...

Read on!

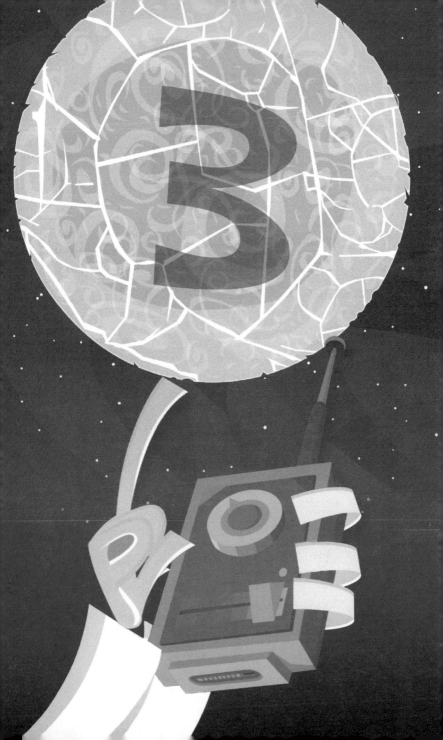

DESTINATION SUN

CHAPTER 3
DESTINATION: ~~FUN~~ *Sun*

Top U.Z.Z. Agent **ANITA KNIGHT** is exactly where she likes to be – in the driving seat. Anita is patiently awaiting instruction from her partner in crime solving – **VICTOR VOLT!**

Victor sits in the passenger seat, a vast map of the cosmos unfolded in his lap.
"Go straight ahead," says Victor. "**ABOUT 150 MILLION KILOMETRES.**"
"Then what?" asks Anita.
"That's it," says Victor.
"Fair enough," says Anita, punching a few buttons on the dashboard. "Plotting course." A **PINGING** sound lets her know that, whatever she's just done, she's done it right. "Course set. Look out Sun, here we come!"

Anita turns the key in the ignition. The rocket engine makes a noise like a woolly mammoth with a terrible cold clearing his trunk in the morning – before dying out (like a mammoth) with a wheezy cough.

"I said, 'Look out Sun, here we come'!" says Anita, turning the key in the ignition.

The engine makes a **spluttering** noise, like someone sighing through their mouth without opening their lips.

And roars into life!

ROOOAAA-

HOORAY!

Then dies out with
a strangulated gasp.

Anita and Victor share a glance, before
turning ahead to face the rocket's windscreen
once again. Anita taps the dashboard for good
luck and turns the key.

There's no doubt about it this time. The
engines have sparked, they're juiced up and
turning over and ready to boost this baby to
the Sun! Well, not a baby as such. Actually
more like...

...a glacier.

Yes, this is one ship
that won't be in any
danger from colliding
with an iceberg – this
spaceship *already* is an

ICEBERG!

Top Agents
VICTOR VOLT
and **ANITA KNIGHT** are about to take off into space – in a rocket-powered **LUMP OF ICE!** Now if only they were heading for a planet-sized glass of fizzy pop then all would be well – but, of course, they're actually on a vitally **important mission** to re-ignite the Sun! And the fate of our dear planet Earth is in their hands!

(So let's hope Victor's got rid of those nasty **shakes** he's had since he wiped out on his **Sky Bike,** earlier.)

27

And so, blasting off from a top secret U.Z.Z. location, the glacier *rocket* shoots off into the sky – with the switched-off Sun in its sights.

Space – a barren place at the best of times – is **gloomier** than ever with the Sun much diminished. Still, Victor and Anita's hearts are full of hope – and their stomachs are a little queasy – as the glacier rocket ricochets dizzyingly around the Moon...

Vrooms past Venus...

And mad dashes by Mercury.

"Are you sure we can land on the Sun in this thing?" queries Victor.

"It is true," pipes up **DOCTOR DOCTOR**, "that this is

totally untested and *highly dangerous!"*

Victor looks around at the blue-faced, snaggle-toothed Doctor.
"Who asked you?" says Victor.
She shrugs (as much as she is able to shrug, being **tied to a chair**).

DOCTOR DOCTOR looks around at the two U.Z.Z. Agents flanking her.
"Huh," mutters **DOCTOR DOCTOR**. "And I thought we were all friends here!"

"**WE ARE**," smiles Anita, as pleasantly as she can muster while talking to her old arch-enemy while hurtling towards the Sun in an interplanetary glacier,

"FRIENDS WHO DON'T TRUST EACH OTHER."

Just then, a **penguin** hops out from behind a block of ice.

Victor and Anita are understandably surprised by the sudden appearance of this flightless, marine diving bird.

(after all, it is commonly found in the colder waters of the Southern Hemisphere but not usually in space).

"Hm," muses Anita. "I guess this is one of the drawbacks of having a chunk of **Antarctica** for a spaceship."

"He might make a **tasty snack**," snickers **DOCTOR DOCTOR**, "since it's unlikely that there will be a service station on the way to the Sun."

Anita tuts at **DOCTOR DOCTOR'S** typically horrid comments and gives the penguin a pat and coos,

"Don't worry little fella, I won't let that mean blue lady hurt you!"

CHAPTER 4
WALKING ON THE SUN

DOCTOR DOCTOR, arch-enemy of U.Z.Z. and Agent of T.H.E.M., is working together with U.Z.Z.'s Top Agents **ANITA KNIGHT** and **VICTOR VOLT** to guide their glacier rocket to a safe landing spot on the surface of the Sun.

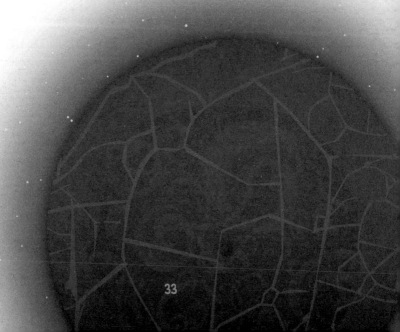

"Okay," says **DOCTOR DOCTOR**, looking out of the window from the chair to which she is tied, "turn left at that Sunspot then take a right at that SOLAR FLARE."

Anita works various levers, carefully bringing down the landing gear.
"**BULLS EYE!**" says **DOCTOR DOCTOR** as the unusual spaceship touches down on the Sun's barren surface.

Anita unsnaps her safety belt. She stands up and takes a well-earned stretch.
"Right," she says,

"LET'S SAVE THE WORLD."

Victor looks out of the window at the scorched surface of the Sun, still glowing dimly.

"Well, at least the weather is good," he jokes. "Sunny, I mean."

Anita rolls her eyes and hands Victor a large bundle of clothes.

"Why don't you slip into something cool," she says, "Like this refrigerator suit."

Victor and Anita make a quick change into the special gear. As soon as they're done they resemble nothing more than a pair of

GIANT
REFRIGERATORS

– complete with novelty magnets and a "To do" list.

"We have exactly half an hour to relight the Sun and get the heck out of here," Anita says, "before our **SPACESHIP** MELTS.

"But what shall we do about her?" asks Victor, nodding in the direction of **DOCTOR DOCTOR**. "You two – keep an eye on her," says Anita, to the two U.Z.Z. Agents.

SHE WON'T MOVE A MUSCLE.

"I'll be as frozen as ice," smiles **DOCTOR DOCTOR**.

Anita jabs a button and a door in the side of the glacier rocket pops open with the sound of a granny taking out her false teeth.

A mechanical whine indicates that a set of stairs are unfolding down to the Sun's **scorched surface.** Victor stands in the doorway of the glacier rocket, contemplating the charred, crusty Sunscape.

"To think," Victor ponders, "I, Victor Volt, will be the first man to walk on the Sun."

I was the first woman!

yells **DOCTOR DOCTOR**, still safely tied up inside the ship.

That's what they'll remember.

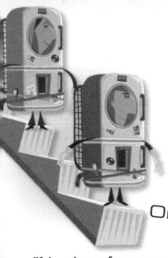

Victor ignores her. "This is one small step for –" And then he falls down the stairs.

Or was he pushed?

"No time for speeches, Victor!" says Anita, bounding down the stairs.

Victor jumps up, rubbing his behind.

"Oo-ow! Burny! Sun! Hot!"

Then he starts hopping from one foot to the other. **"SHOES! MELT!"** he yelps.

Victor shouts into his Communicator. "Come in, Professor Professor! **Oo-ee!** This is Victor Volt! **YOW!** I need help!"

Through a burst of static, **SPECIAL AGENT RAY'S** face appears on Victor's Communicator.

"Sorry!" pipes Ray. "Professor Professor's having a 'tinkle'. But he left a message: 'if you overheat, activate the booster cooling systems'."

"Eee!

Booster cooling systems!

Yargh!

What 'booster cooling systems'?

Aiee!"

squawks Victor.

"The chunk-ah chunk-ah ice maker!" sighs Ray, trying to put it in terms Victor might understand.

Victor looks down at the front of his refrigerator suit and presses a large button.

CHUNK-AH! CHUNK-AH! CHUNK-AH!
CHUNK-AH! CHUNK-AH!

Chunks of ice flow out of the front of Victor's refrigerator suit, cooling down his hot feet.

CHUNK-AH! CHUNK-AH!

CHUNK-AH!

CHUNK-AH!

CHUNK-AH!

"Aaah," sighs Victor.
"Much better!"

Anita sparks up her Communicator.

"Doctor Doctor," she says, "as you've been here before, perhaps you could tell us – where is the tunnel to the centre of the Sun?"

DOCTOR DOCTOR'S voice comes crackling over Anita's Communicator.

"Just a couple of metres to your right –"

Eeeeedddddarrrrrgggghhhh!

"Ah," says Anita. "It's alright. Victor's found it already."

Anita looks down the hole.

"**VICTOR**," she says.

"**ARE YOU STILL ALIVE?**"

"*I think so!*" he says.

CHAPTER 5
THERE IS A LIGHT THAT SOMETIMES GOES OUT

VICTOR VOLT and **ANITA KNIGHT** are walking down a tunnel to the centre of the Sun – they have left their arch-enemy **DOCTOR DOCTOR** behind in their glacier rocket, with a couple of U.Z.Z. Agents and a penguin. (And it's doubtful that you'll read a **stranger sentence** than that any time today.)

"You know, anyone could have broken that **Remote Control**," moans Victor.

"Oh no, not this again," mutters Anita.
"The **real villain** is the person who made the remote control that controls the Sun. Remotely," says Victor. "Right?"
Anita stops dead in her tracks. With her hands on her hips, she squares up to Victor and stares him straight in the eye. "Did you step on it?" asks Anita, matter-of-factly.
Victor pauses before answering, "Yes."
"Now, **get over it!**" barks Anita, marching ahead, determined that they solve the task in hand.

Meanwhile, back in the glacier rocket... The two U.Z.Z. Agents are frozen solid in blocks of ice! And **DOCTOR DOCTOR** is no longer tied to her chair!

"No one **ever** searches your ears," cackles
DOCTOR DOCTOR, wiping the earwax from her
mini-freeze freeze-ray ray gun.
She makes her way over to the dashboard
and begins tinkering about with the controls.
"Now," she says, "I wonder how
this thing works..."

DOCTOR DOCTOR doesn't
realize it – but two beady
penguin eyes peer timidly
from behind a chair...

While **DOCTOR DOCTOR** fiddles, the Sun's pilot light burns. Or not, as the case may be. "There," says Victor, with not inconsiderable awe.

"The centre of the Sun!"

"Doctor Doctor helped us find our way here," says Anita. "She really is on our side, after all!"

"Right," says Victor, pushing up a sleeve. "You read the instructions. Let's see if we can kick start this thing and get it re-ignited."

"OK," says Anita, reading the instructions helpfully set out at the Sun's core. "One. Flip roto-ignition to the 'almost on' position. Two. Click the missing switch behind the placebo vent. Three…"

"Wait a minute," says Victor, "roto-what?"

Over at the glacier rocket, **DOCTOR DOCTOR**
claps her bony hands and clacks her teeth.
"If they only knew how badly I was about to
double cross them!" she cackles.

WHU-HUH-HUH-HUH-HER-HER-HER-HA-HAAA!"

DOCTOR DOCTOR turns the key in the ignition.
The rocket engine makes a noise like a bag of
spanners being thrown down a stone staircase
– before **clanking** back to silence.

"Stupid piece of **junk**," grumbles the Doctor
– giving the dashboard a good kick.

A large piece of ice drops off the outside of the
spaceship, and splashes down into the ever-
growing puddle outside.

DOCTOR DOCTOR taps the dashboard for good luck and turns the key. This time the ship's engines roar into life…

RRRAAAOOORRRGGGHHH

Down in the centre of the Sun, Anita is reading out the last of the instructions. "Twenty five," she says. "Press red button to light."

Victor presses the red button.

NOTHING HAPPENS.

He presses it again.

NOTHING HAPPENS AGAIN.

He presses it and holds it down.

He gives it a succession of quick little taps.

He bashes it with his fist.

NOTHING HAPPENS SEVERAL TIMES.

"Okay," Victor frowns. "We're **doomed.**"
"Victor," says Anita, through clenched teeth.
"We have ten minutes before our spaceship
melts."
Anita's Communicator crackles into life.

"Hello, everyone!" announces
DOCTOR DOCTOR. "How's it going?"

"We've tried everything," says Victor, "and
nothing will light the Sun!"

"Did you try this?"

says **DOCTOR DOCTOR**...

PLOOOF!

The pilot light suddenly *bursts* into flame – just what Victor and Anita had been struggling to do! "How did you do that?" says Victor, gobsmacked.

"**TA-DAH!**" says **DOCTOR DOCTOR** over the Communicator. She holds up the remote control that controls the Sun. Remotely.

Victor punches the air. "Yesss!" says Victor, triumphantly. "I knew it wasn't **my fault**!"

"**SUCKERS!**" gloats the Doctor. "The remote control Victor broke wasn't the real one! I switched them! I had it all along! "WHU-HUH-HUH-HUH-HER-HER-HER-HA-HAAA!"

"Yesss!" shouts Victor triumphantly. "I knew it wasn't **my fault!**"

"Victor!" shouts Anita.

"WE'RE ALL goiNg To DiE!"

"Sorry," Victor says, in a very small voice.

"It was such a simple trap!" **DOCTOR DOCTOR** goes on, mesmerized by her own brilliance. "I fooled you with the old 'broken remote control' gag, tricked you into taking me on this rocket-powered iceberg, let you go to the centre of the Sun, and now I just have to relight the Sun and fly away to safety *while you get fried!*" **DOCTOR DOCTOR** spins a dial on her remote control.

The Sun's pilot light blooms into a big, tasty-looking flame, instantly beginning to re-ignite the Sun to its full glory. Victor starts freaking out.

"Oo-ow! Burny!"

he shouts.

"Yow! Yargh! Hot!"

He hops from one foot to another, frantically pressing his button and trying to activate the chunk-ah chunk-ah ice maker.

"Don't bother," says Anita, coolly. She hands Victor the end of a rope. "Just hold this," she says. "Very, very tightly."

Victor takes hold of the end of the rope and says, "What do you want me to hold this fooo ooooooooooooooooooooooooooooooooooooooooo oooooooooooooooooooooooooooooooooooo oooooooooooooooooooooooooooooooo oooooooooooooooooooooooooooooooo oooooooooooooooooooooooooooooo ooooooooooooooooooooooooooo ooooooooooooooooooooooooo oooooooOOOOOOOr…?"

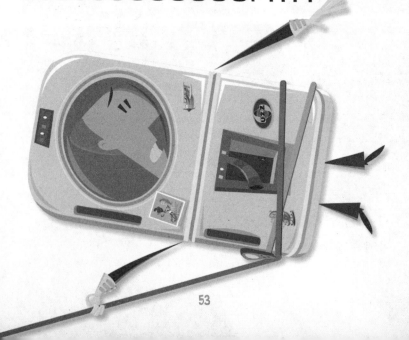

CHAPTER 6
WHO INVITED THE PENGUIN?

As the Sun re-ignites, a vast *ball of flame* tears up the corridors down which Top U.Z.Z. Agents **ANITA KNIGHT** and **VICTOR VOLT** just walked a moment ago...

and just metres ahead of this flame, Anita and Victor are dragged through the air by a rope... a rope that is attached to...

the melting glacier rocket...

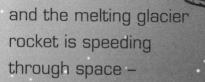

and the melting glacier rocket is speeding through space –

BACK TOWARDS EARTH!

And on-board the melting glacier rocket
speeding back towards Earth, are two frozen
U.Z.Z. Agents, an evil double-crossing Doctor...

And...

a penguin!

"Victory is mine!" cackles **DOCTOR DOCTOR**,
triumphantly – before being dive-bombed
by a penguin.

"**AIEE!**" shrieks **DOCTOR DOCTOR**. "Get off me
you stout-bodied, short-legged, flightless bird!"

DOCTOR DOCTOR wrestles the penguin to the
ground. But the penguin rapidly gains the upper
flipper (or, to be more precise, flipper-like wing).
The penguin produces a soggy wet fish and
uses it to **SLAP** DOCTOR DOCTOR about the
shoulders.

"Stop it! Stop it!" screeches **DOCTOR DOCTOR**, "You eater of **krill**, **FISH** and **small squid!**" She grabs the penguin's beak and pulls...

THE PENGUIN'S HEAD...

CLEAN

OFF!

"Professor?" gawps **DOCTOR DOCTOR**.

"ZAT'S PROFESSOR PROFESSOR TO YOU!" says the penguin-suited **PROFESSOR PROFESSOR**, pinning **DOCTOR DOCTOR** to the ground. "HA HA!" crows **PROFESSOR PROFESSOR** triumphantly, "I FINALLY HAVE YOU VERE I VANT YOU!"

"But you don't have this!" says **DOCTOR DOCTOR**, brandishing the **REMOTE CONTROL**.

PROFESSOR PROFESSOR grabs the remote control – and **SMASHES** it to smithereens!

Yay!

But **DOCTOR DOCTOR** holds up another one. "That was a fake!" brags **DOCTOR DOCTOR**.

PROFESSOR PROFESSOR grabs the second remote control – and **DASHES** it to pieces!

Alright!

But **DOCTOR DOCTOR** holds up another one.

"That was a fake!" boasts **DOCTOR DOCTOR**.

PROFESSOR PROFESSOR grabs the third
remote control – and **TURNS** it into toast!

Hurrah!

But **DOCTOR DOCTOR** holds up
another one.
"That was a fake!" swanks
DOCTOR DOCTOR.

This carries on for a while...

**YOU CAN
USE YOUR
IMAGINATION...**

Until Victor and Anita enter – having hauled
themselves along the rope and into the spaceship
– and appear in the cab of the glacier rocket.

They stand and watch the wrestling for a while. It's not often you see a Doctor and a Professor, in a penguin suit, fighting over a series of fake remote controls.

Eventually **DOCTOR DOCTOR** hands a remote control to Anita. "Hold this for me, for a minute," says **DOCTOR DOCTOR**. But then she realizes what she's done.

THAT WAS THE REAL ONE.

SMECK!

A fish **SLAPS DOCTOR DOCTOR** across the face. "Time," gasps the Doctor, "out!" And she collapses to the ground.

Anita and **PROFESSOR PROFESSOR** cheer and hug each other. But Victor stands aloof. He has something on his mind.

"What are you doing here?" he asks **PROFESSOR PROFESSOR**. Victor looks at Anita. "Why wasn't I told about this?" he asks.

PROFESSOR PROFESSOR and Anita look at each other. **"SECRET!"** they both say at once!

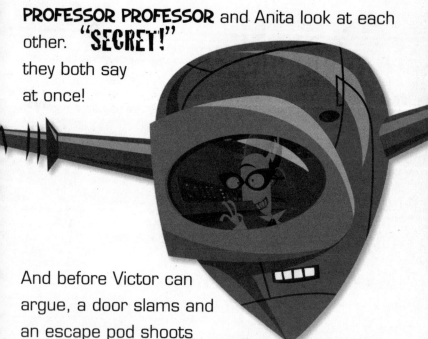

And before Victor can argue, a door slams and an escape pod shoots past the window...

OooPS!

EPILOGUE:
THE SUN HAS BEEN SWITCHED BACK ON, HIP-HIP HIP-HIP HOORAY!

"So Doctor Doctor made a clean escape," says **CHANGED DAILY** – sorry, **Oinky Doinky** – from his favourite spot, leaning on the mantelpiece. "But at least it's a sunny day."

"AND WE HAVE ZE REMOTE CONTROL!" says **PROFESSOR PROFESSOR**.

"Don't we?" Victor and Anita look at each other. They both shrug.

"VICTOR!" says the **PROFESSOR PROFESSOR**.

"DO YOU HAVE ZE REMOTE?"

"I did have," says Victor. "A moment ago."

"CHECK DOWN ZE SIDE OF ZE CHAIRS!" says **PROFESSOR PROFESSOR**. "ZAT IS WHAT ALWAYS HAPPENS TO ME AT HOME."

Victor and Anita step
out of their chairs.

CRUNCH!

Victor has trodden on
the remote control.
Again.

And everything
turns to...

BLACK.

THE END.
(Forever!)

Doctor Doctor gleefully presses the button on her remote control and turns off the sun.

She presses it again and turns the sun back on. And off. And on. In the struggle to snatch the remote control, Victor, um, steps on it. Ooops.

Professor Professor has no idea how to fix the remote control and turn the sun back on.

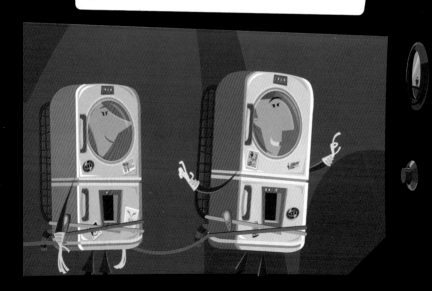

Working together with Doctor Doctor, Victor and Anita journey to the centre of the sun to relight the pilot light.

When Victor and Anita are at the sun's core, Doctor Doctor brandishes the remote control and turns on the sun!

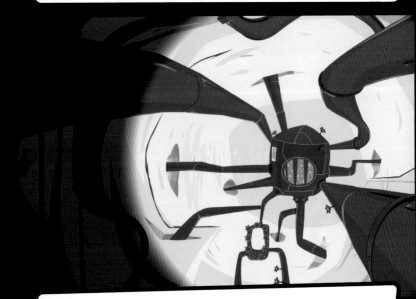

As the sun roars back to life, Victor and Anita make a quick getaway to the iceberg spaceship.